THIS BOOK BELONGS TO:

Penny

I Love You!

Karen Clinch

Published by Tate Publishing & Enterprises, LLC
127 E. Trade Center Terrace | Mustang, Oklahoma 73064 USA
1.888.361.9473 | www.tatepublishing.com

Tate Publishing is committed to excellence in the publishing industry. The company reflects the philosophy established by the founders, based on Psalm 68:11,
"The Lord gave the word and great was the company of those who published it."

Book design copyright © 2008 by Tate Publishing, LLC. All rights reserved.
Cover design & interior design by Elizabeth A. Mason
Illustration by Jeff Elliott

Published in the United States of America

ISBN: 978-1-60462-830-2
1. Youth & Children   2. Christian: Fiction: Poetry
3. Ages 0-5
08.02.12

PEEK-A-BOO
MOON

karen clinch

TATE PUBLISHING & Enterprises

DEDICATION

To Mom and Dad, for memories saved; pictures in my heart engraved. And to my children, though we're often apart; you keep your mother young at heart.

ACKNOWLEDGMENTS

Friends at Helvetia Community Church who encouraged me to go beyond my comfort zone, I thank you! Melody and Kimmie, you encouraged me to persevere, and I pray blessings on you. To my soul-mate husband who understands me more than any person on earth, and to my awesome Father God who puts dreams in my heart, inspiration in my path, and then follows through with the words to express all I feel inside, my never-ending love.

FOREWORD

Many years ago, when I was three or four years old, my mother took us on a road trip to Oregon. It wasn't unusual for us to travel. We lived in California, and my mother's family lived in Oregon. We used to go often to visit them, and my brother and I loved getting up very early in the morning—while it was still dark outside—to set out on our long trip. This particular ride, however, was very dark. It was a stormy night, and as we traveled, I couldn't go to sleep as usual, because there were no lights anywhere, and I was frightened. My mother sensed my fear, and as we drove along she consoled me. About that time the moon came out from behind the clouds, and knowing I was almost in tears, Mom said, "Peek-a-Boo! The moon came out to say hello to you!" It made me laugh, and as I watched the moon go in and out of the clouds, I finally fell asleep. My mother has blended that story, along with a few memories of beloved camping experiences in her childhood, to create this playful story I know everyone will enjoy.

—Kimberly Colon, daughter of the author.

Fragrance of pine, smoke from the fire, tables laid out in picnic attire. Backpacks unloaded, the family all here.
Giggles and chatter heard everywhere.
We all set up camp in our own special way. The grown-ups talked, and the children played. Mom prepared dinner on campfire's flame. Daytime was fading to night's twilight gray.

Sitting around the campfire's warmth,
tummies all filled with marshmallow smores.
Story time telling 'neath dark cloudy skies,
voices now softened, set low for the night.

Mom made sure the mosquitoes wouldn't bite as she zipped up our bags and tucked us in tight. Mine lay beneath a big Douglas fir. I chose the outdoors—gave my tent to the girls.

Dad made his rounds of hugs and prayers then tended the fire
with tedious care. A smile goodnight as he went to his tent
and left me alone, quite cozy, content.

Owls were hooting, embers cracking, breezes whispering in the trees. Crickets were chirping, and I could hear the rippling rapids of a nearby stream. Nighttime noises unfamiliar, how could a body rest? Imagination running wild. Heart pounding in my chest. Eyes so heavy, wanting sleep, but choosing not to close, lest something out there I should miss—I dare not even doze.

Is that a bear? Was that a bat? Do I see this? Did I hear that?
The dark plays tricks on a young camper's mind,
but it must never show.
Stick it out, show courage bravely, and battle every foe.

One. . . two. . . three. . .

I'll try to count some sheep.
But I'm no closer now than I was, to sleep.

Four. . . five. . . six. . .

they just aren't here! Sheep don't come when they sense your fea

Then a pleasant sight appeared. The moon came out to say hello.
Shown down to lighten the darkest crevice with its illuminating
glow. Its friendly light brought comfort—its smiling face delight.
Recognizing familiar things brought peace to restless night.

I saw the clouds go speeding by, silver-tipped treetops
towering high.
The outline of our family's cars shone brightly
by light from a thousand stars.
The tent tops glistened with nighttime dew.
Coming from them was a snore or two.
I was glad I'd chosen to sleep outside under
the moon and stars tonight.

The eerie night sounds quieted, and I thought that I could hear the shining moon whisper to my heart, "Be still and do not fear. I'll stay with you awhile, and I will be your friend. I'll lighten up your

About that time a cloud came by to muffle the quiet voice.
Then passed as quickly as it came.
Hide-and-Seek was Moon's game of choice.
For just a minute or maybe two a cloud would cover Moon's
fullness. Then he'd pop out, say "Peek-a-boo!" and glow again with
brilliance. With each little cloud that floated past, he helped me
learn the dark won't last. I learned to wait, tried not to fret,
until the light came back again.

We played our game, who knows how long? It calmed my fear, helped my heart grow strong. I liked this game. I had such fun. But would my friend fade with the rise of the sun?
"Please don't go. I like you here.
When your light shines, I have no fear."

"It isn't the moon that brings you peace," just then I heard him say.
"But rather the Father's only Son to whom you owe your praise.
He sent me here to comfort you so you might know his love.
He watches you each night and day from the heavens up above.
Good night, my friend.
Now go to sleep. My time tonight has ended. His message
delivered to your heart is what he had intended."

I lay there thinking for a moment or two about all that I had heard. Dad's earlier prayer ran through my mind. I recalled most every word. Dad had prayed to a loving God to keep me safe tonight. My eyes gave way to heaviness and

The black bird squawked out his alarm to
welcome in the day, but I knew I
had somehow changed and would never
be the same. A little bit wiser I'd become.
Through dark of night I'd met God's Son.

No longer would I fear the darkness when drifting off to sleep.
Praying to He who guides moon and stars
was better than counting sheep.
A New Beginning, and never The End,
when the Heavenly Father becomes your friend.

e|LIVE

listen|imagine|view|experience

AUDIO BOOK DOWNLOAD INCLUDED WITH THIS BOOK!

In your hands you hold a complete digital entertainment package. Besides purchasing the paper version of this book, this book includes a free download of the audio version of this book. Simply use the code listed below when visiting our website. Once downloaded to your computer, you can listen to the book through your computer's speakers, burn it to an audio CD or save the file to your portable music device (such as Apple's popular iPod) and listen on the go!

How to get your free audio book digital download:

1. Visit www.tatepublishing.com and click on the e|LIVE logo on the home page.
2. Enter the following coupon code:
   732c-9790-6e50-217c-547b-2615-3b72-9daa
3. Download the audio book from your e|LIVE digital locker and begin enjoying your new digital entertainment package today!